ISABEL PIN

When I Grow Up,
I Will Win the Nobel Peace Prize

Translated from the German by Nancy Seitz

FARRAR, STRAUS AND GIROUX

When I grow up, I will love my neighbor.

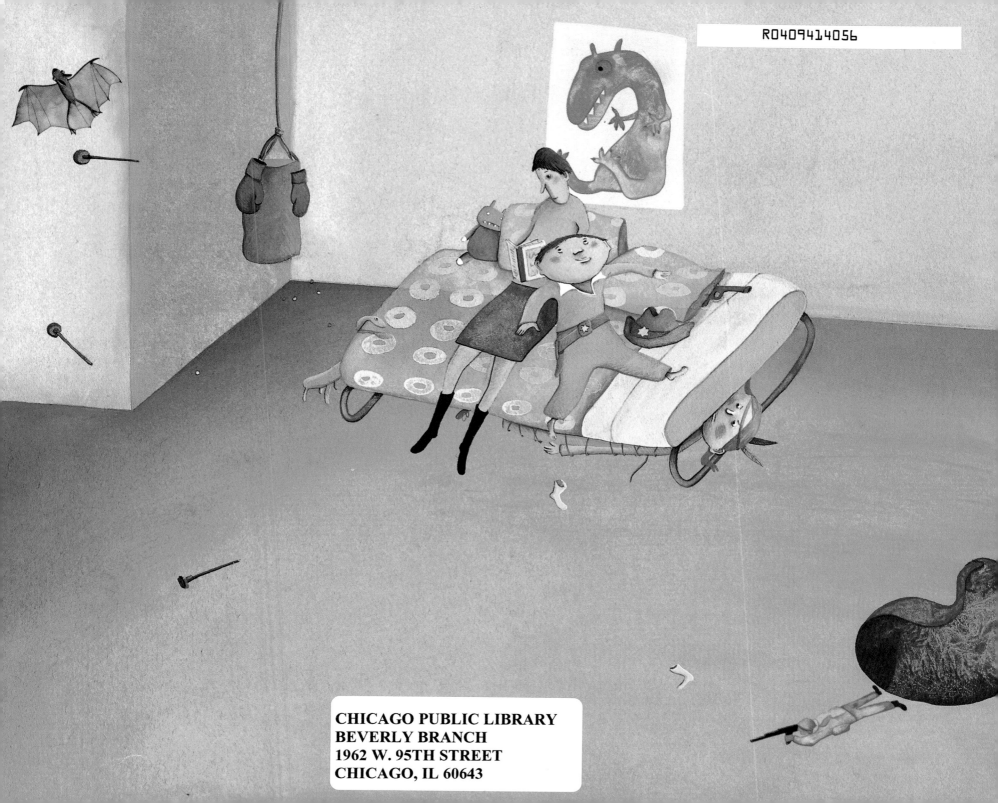

I will create peace in the world and among all people.

I will save animals from cruelty.

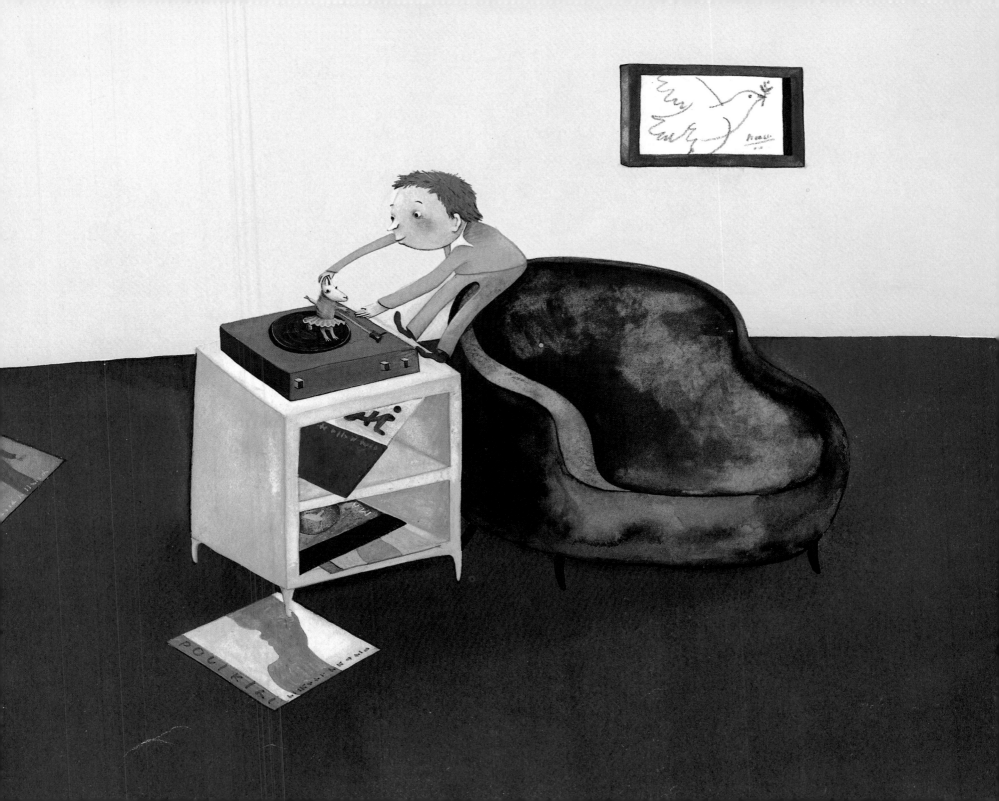

I will share with the poor and the unfortunate.

I will protect the environment and help save our planet.

I will give aid to people who need it.

I will not tolerate injustice or greed.

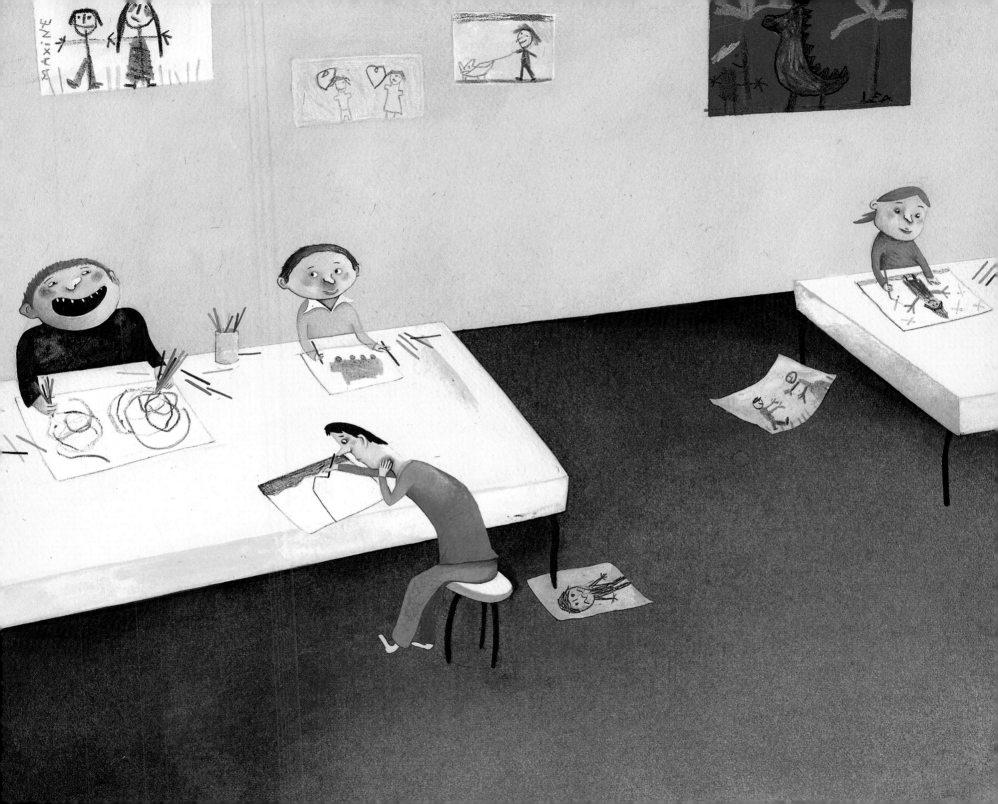

I will be brave in difficult situations.

I will achieve great things, and the most distinguished people in the world will give me the Nobel Peace Prize.

There's so much to do. I ought to get started right away.

THE NOBEL PEACE PRIZE

Awarded yearly since 1901, the Nobel Prize was established by Alfred Nobel (1833–1896), a Swedish chemist, inventor, and industrialist who received over three hundred patents in his lifetime and made a fortune from his most famous invention, dynamite. As stipulated in his will, most of Nobel's estate was used to establish a fund from which prizes would be awarded in his name for those who had done "the most or the best work" for peace, as well as for those whose achievements in physiology or medicine, chemistry, physics, and literature had "conferred the greatest benefit on mankind." A prize for economics was added in 1969.

Recipients of the Nobel Peace Prize include Jean Henri Dunant (1901 / French founder of the Red Cross), Jane Addams (1931 / U.S. feminist and social worker), Martin Luther King, Jr. (1964 / U.S. civil rights leader), Doctors Without Borders (1999 / Belgian medical relief organization), and Wangari Maathai (2004 / Kenyan environmental and political leader). The three Nobel Peace Laureates represented in this book are (from left to right on page 23): the Fourteenth Dalai Lama, Tenzin Gyatso (1989 / Tibetan religious leader), Nelson Mandela (1993 / South African civil rights leader), and Mother Teresa (1979 / Indian missionary).

For more information about the Nobel Prize, visit the official Web site: http://nobelprize.org.

www.fsgkidsbooks.com

Library of Congress Control Number: 2005929316

ISBN-13: 978-0-374-38313-8
ISBN-10: 0-374-38313-8